# SWANOCEROSMAN TWO

*by*

## Joseph Mondrella

DORRANCE PUBLISHING CO
EST. 1920
PITTSBURGH, PENNSYLVANIA 15238

Dorrance Publishing Co
585 Alpha Drive
Pittsburgh, PA 15238
Visit our website at www.dorrancebookstore.com

ISBN: 979-8-8872-9329-5
eISBN: 979-8-8872-9829-0

# SWANOCEROSMAN TWO

*by*

**Joseph Mondrella**

## PROLOGUE: GOOD-HEARTED GOOD STARTED

Knowing darn well that what they were dangerous innocentlier than so's the Cartel, before the long journey of returning it wasn't going to be a disaster unalike the dang Hindenberg. After their heart-to-heart which wasn't hard to start, what was more choice 'n' joyous than listening to a fiddler's that for Goosepotamuswoman's corps, in the moment's split spur; getting a night's sleep was within the mountainous area's miniature lake's inselberg. Goosepotamuswoman knew what was of use similar to a suiting to-be-dried towel, it was that for the first time in too long she was able to sleep with Swanocerosman cheek by jowl. The second they woke up to the genies who weren't meanies like they were the crew's alarm clock's when they were notified about how new entanglements was a matter of acceptance for those strengthened by the school of hardknocks. Loosely speaking, the alarmers' offer's what led them into unchartered, grim waters. Mentally relaxed and in tact, they hadn't at all yet wanted to live a life not action-packed. What the ligergiraffe was along with not soft is on the ball like some friends or like hawks're, he wasn't off his trolley when he found out his love life was what he could iron out come hell or high water. When they realized their chances didn't have to get great, their clan insisted the prize'd outweigh dead weight. Only the ligergiraffe was granted a custom parachute to use after enough of a free fall, it wasn't like being in the path of a wrecking ball, on the double; when it comes to the bubble of theirs it very much seemed like not a soul'd pop the bubble. It was sure what they were on the verge of doin' was what couldn't be pulled the damn plug on, unalike capped-up porous wrecks they felt like a tyrannosaurus rex trying to eat a bullied mastodon. They hadn't noticed a message that's in Braille, although it'll be a bitch unalike a passage, railed, not named Abigail, when it came to their newfound cause that ship hadn't sailed. Ready for it all like a corp's herd's tower, souls'd end up so dead much like what died for a quarter pounder. How they weren't automatically spankedly-cursed so's true as how one who people've praised so is Allah, out and about as well as hardcorer too, for them things were about to get pretty crazy sure like things had during World War Two in Okinawa. They enchantedly gazed upon the realm they've wound up in like a star counter, ready to get physical like a bar's bouncer. On a total win streak unlike the recipient of a medal which without being covered in colors couldn't be along with more of a whitey bronzer, they've been familiar with the mightiest mightiness like the almighty father.

Dragon Fliper

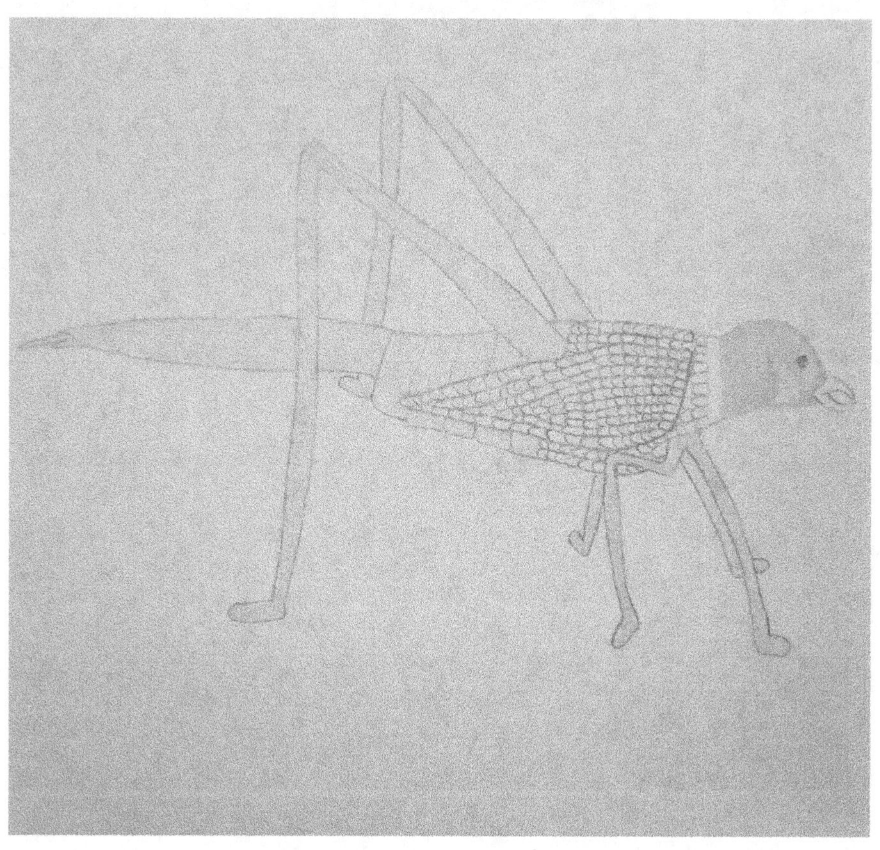

Pheasant-Headed Timid Cricket

Large Pitbull Cardinal

Hound Hawk Groundhogs

## CHAPTER ONE:
## THE FREAKIN' SCARY BEINGS' PRAIRIE

Down's how they hovered, they anticipated somethin' excitin' comin' like a hungry person who all the way out found a cupboard. They couldn't make out what the organisms beneath were like they were in an aircraft, but then they were dealt admittance not from an airshaft. To them the huge prairie was a reality unalike the Tooth Fairy. What was true was how it doesn't rain in Jan., was still why they were able to straight withstand what wasn't chewed Raisin Bran, fries that're along with hot, sought-curly, or what's served plus sure eaten during a hot dog tourney. They had gotten 'round without mountain bikes, if you'd say what they mustn't do is continue, just to remain honest you'd have to follow up with what's sound is sike's. When life's a bitch that's no cockapoo, their limbs're born to fly like a cockatoo. No matter what a cold world'd dish low blows, so at least they'll always have the most valuable around like pro bowls. It's not like they were going to get co-ordinates or shepherd's pies yet they'd need exercise, so like tantra, when forces try to treat them worse than fibromyalgia. The trumped young weren't placed in low enclosures, when they ended up dead as some ageless organ donors. The sternestly, they in defense because of foe-units, turned them into what for the rest of eternity yep's post-humous. They knew there was a debt to collect from living in a style that is ultimately abroad without cars, courts, plus quads; unlike a silliness, their willingness marked no facades. This was a quest for fulfilment to the alphas slash fullest, to prove the alpha-clan's goldest. If you could solve all the problems the world tosses your way, you'd be well off, so they let what would bug get set up without having to get Off. The difference was scarier than a mini germ's bod, for getting too territorial like the Wermacht. Tapping into what those alike would like which was no stemmed peapod, was more precious or bestest, relative to a forget-me-not. Nobody got finished by smallpox, they were finishing each other unlike malt pops. What had their attention obviously wasn't 3D movies, chasers, or freaking movie trailers; the ligergiraffe and Goosepotamus-woman's bites never came with pao, kung, so far those that felt them all ate crap different from what's name is cow dung. Swanocerosman's horn was niftier to him than a funnel straight in use, they've made the numbers look like who wears when around funnel cakes big shoes. First thing they were hostilely greeted by dragon flypers that were finished off easily like appetizers, not one sunken fang, bein' gifted less rustiness from such must-bes is why the happening was just a fantastic example of yin yang. To act leglessly and brainlessly was sure not in their greatest interest, their makers they met and could no longer be resenting were forced to be clenching like a big hitter's fist. All ready to relax like a dead-daytime sermon's persons or as if they grabbed an offered weed bowl, they were spotted by yes way kind vermin persons who took them to a watering hole. They weren't going to pass up reciprocating their new lads' chivalry, they appreciated it like a tourist would end up appreciating visiting Italy. They were in less of a rush than when Goosepotamuswoman had to be rescued so they figured they could use unalike the word that did shoosh, which is "Sh," chill pills. It wasn't a bad option choosing to sit still given that they felt to revel it wouldn't take being willing to level with bills that aren't platypuses' bills. They were tons of peas in a pod all night until the vermin persons introduced a discrepancy, what had happened turned out to be a sneak attack on the ligergiraffe whom is far more ruthless than any chick whose name is Stephanie. Soon as the ligergiraffe started yawning, one of the vermin persons failed at throwing an arrowhead spear dead at his head although it uplifted his mood in his mane; his roar woke Swanocerosman and Goosepotamuswoman fast enough to fight off whose true colors weren't a pretty sight like binge-eating taco sauce or picturin' the Holocaust, by in mind sightin' people that were Jewish's train. The coyote vermin person was the one to turn on them in order to grant his clan ligergiraffe meals, they instead felt what was near that ligergiraffe's heels. What the vermin persons separately were like was a half termite, half coyote, a half mouse, half rat, half weasel, and half cockroach; when in deep destiny knew Swanocerosman and his friends getting primed by such primetime wasn't half-bad like a stony-made slash wowed-at and regal, rad damn rock porch. When they were chilling with the backstabbers, they found out about their out-of-this-world-as-a-couple-gas-Saturns hill cave, which they've ended up locating plus pillaging for its gas lanterns. Why they gladly fancied, that's not because of along with all-rolled wheat/cheese wraps, Dots, a fat camp, sagged belt, and niacin although; strong headlamps as well as night vision goggles. Once the coast was clear without getting the chance to pour some beer, the ligergiraffe then feasted on the hound hawk groundhogs; meanwhile, Swanocerosman along with Goosepotamuswoman plus their storkupine did stomach what is less faux than Velcro; like in addition to legs o' taken out chomped frogs, propane-grilled, browned hotdogs. Not doin' bad like a sure-fed country's providence, the ligergiraffe had to swat dead the cave's guards which were hound hawk groundhogs, once he gained an allied greater sense of reconnaissance. Even bein' not bad news like the not-so-wild straight-liked slash sweet mid of fall, to him spanking the fresh-trumped ranking of out of bounds hound hawk groundhogs was child's play like playing wiffleball. The non-void four's circle stood where nothing scared old heads, not where boys or girls could find plus keep arrowheads. What they gave each other was deeper than was telling somebody cheers, or amid a shot photo giving your pal with your fingers bunny ears. They'd want each other's wraths which were smooth as clockwork, around more than some birdbaths, a shop clerk, Caribbean jerk, or some living-big Turk. Picking moves was dissimilar to among ducks on a pond a sitting loon, but truly doing so meant being all for fighters like sure, which company along with Windy? Boon. They were only there since what they were fit of in turn's crusades, they'd buy that they'd fight not differed Kool-Aids. To their record they were trying to add wins more than what's thyme, like faced pro Angels that play in Anaheim. Lord knows whoever shall get too territorial towards them'd be drunk on power like skanky brides, who were all behind their men's backs on dating sites. For them being more fit to kill than a pet owner's dear schnauzer, wasn't a thing of the past unalike the bent codeword Sears Tower. They just kept kemptly stepping forward like pro mathematicians, sucked-up dealing much with equations' pleadin' powers; at least they weren't along with so-hatcheted, dissimilar to for how they hadn't had unappreciative tastelessness, sweet 'n' sours. Venturing like Ash Ketchum in some green grass, was for them unalike a liked/dealt-up nicotine patch. What they ended been in isn't spritzes, so they were content the loved sec they were able to make real meals out of pheasant breasted timid crickets. A fate soundin' really not intriguing as keeping a pulled-out-weed, or coldly storing barnacled lard-sicles, was for the warring made-cold, out-plead, packed-flock of mad-probbed large pit bull cardinals. Frowned upon different from Congress' conferences, was showing mercy unalike wife-beaters or mice-eaters to very much coldly-turning monstrous finch ostriches. Of cat gnats plus bobcat wombats, a mantis dragon was not resenting making body-temperature suppers. They pretty much were told it would be worth it like as well as valued shares, cheese; who cared really's who'd dish up coldness which so didn't belong to any Januaries. They had to be smooth, not velvety, also definitely ready to not slip unalike somebody who happened to get mickied. They were after meals more vicious than tamales, since they were told by the genies who weren't meanies fending off souls out where they had been placed wasn't sadistic different from

Nazis. Righteously superstitious like a successful pilot bringing a helicopter that's a Huey back, they'd make their world their home without having to use salad tossers and to weed wack. Lord knows these moments which ensued were for making the most of kind of like some person's pull up bar, or some distributor of dumpsters' old junkyard. What they commanded wasn't golf carts, yet in fact they commanded with more heart on them than a card of hearts. It hadn't even came to mind how the forest they were approachin' would offer soldiers protection from artillery that's aerial, not jarred by a possibility of scars, looks never mattered like Swanocerosman wouldn't ever be impressed by some hardened, turnt, streetman's jerry curl. They were through with the grounds in which they've faced an uncharmin' number of varmints that each were somewhat humanly plus weren't Mickey Mouse or Minnie Mouse; where they were off to its Blendedganisms hadn't got much ruffage from, and some of its inhabitants were about to sight what's worse than two times one busted thumb. After all that is just the reality alike how what a character from Spongebob Squarepants must not get at The Chum Bucket's some plate which is native to the southern-est America; I call them Blendedganisms, since if made into cards in the real world they'd wield words and have something in common with, the way they'd grant eyes comfort, Ms. America. They basically went "bye bye high grass, hi hi dryness," this, they would stay fine by nonchalantly like whom would stay fine by life-size lilacs? wived bride-tigresses.

Monster Finch Ostrich

Bobcat Wombats

Mantis Dragon

Vermin Persons

## CHAPTER TWO:
## A GRAND WASTELAND

With spines, possibly indeed non-in-line inhabitants had much of a chance against them as they out there would to score eveningwear; with a chance slimmer than slim, your bet might've been that somewhere nearby was a public service announcement from Smokey the Bear. The potential of them calling upon bodily action like an in-action drum peddle, was nothin' says how they've noticed they might as well be civil like kids mid the summertime playing foursquare. The Blendedganisms withholdin' from crossin' their challenged thresholds was why Swanocerosman wanted to tell 'em in person "um, pound it," while downright tied to what's outside like a woman sure in some cowprint; either way bein' threatfully needless was the best ol' sweetness exercised religiously much alike say, The Lord's Prayer. If you swiftly had gotten through it the span wasn't a hotspot that had got you bedhead; nothin' indifferent to waking for lovey-dovey cuddlin', it did smell of muscle 'n' ex-livin' deadnesses like any meats put fresh out of a crockpot smack-dab onto French bread. Large sharp-teethed aardvark bees were getting picked off by man-like fly traps, as well as jackrabbit/dragons. Their eyes accidentally locked onto the nearest star then they tried shakin' it off by shaking like in-the-eyehole-sun-touched peeps, and sure, a wet doggy; they seen a coyobra coming after a hedgehoggy hedgedonkey. Sacrifices made agonized individuals mad like the damn globe's sure-raunchy findings, at times fiascos charred longleaf pine trees. They were fortunate the way what was primitive similar to Amish sirs hadn't gotten them cooked as potstickers, toasted bagels, or twin eggrolls. The meanest force couldn't, so wouldn't, be woodland dynamiters; then again survivors did need an environment like non-picked-yet bing cherries, and after the woodland's wildfires, anyone meticulous wouldn't have been ridiculous to have thought somebody that's iniquitous shot incendiaries. The real hot and so grand wasteland's what Swanocerosman carried out no Operation Desert Storm in, but like how he'd hear contact more than hair bands, that's no big deal like when a non-sure-basic feller's Mormon. When it comes to how much blood spilled there was more than two bled three quarts, the reasons were more needed than USB ports. Although the sand dished up red eye the solution was never saline, and picked up dead-right W's is what to winners was sweeter than a praline. Just living out there was harder than to bartend, that to them was simple as how arches bend. The ligergiraffe dominantly was along with a handful, sized-bigger than the standing, daunty, non-respawning mammal-like hissers; therefore, his two best pals were for real more who to then call way brave like some cavalry, after all they would work like a prompting parent trying to catch his mischievous kids by opting to come back early. Much evident is the way messin' with the dang assemblage's power went worse for others than to get hit by a showered hailstone, to break your calf bone, or to accidentally pound your tailbone by butt-first towering towards, downwards flagstone. Non-suiting's calling them less balls-to-the-wall than chainsmokin' tradesfolk, what it was rigged as it gets like given how they were able to fight on's some iPod Touch that's been jailbroke. The beaten couldn't've prevented a thing unalike to plant wheel chocks, at nighttime the night sky got dark because of the moon not more so than sudsy bocks. They couldn't for a fact concernedly have one worry, since they stood all for openings like my dang pad's darn doorknobs, or for lettin' stuff happen somewhat alike pipes faced that are corncobs. Only an inept damn nutjob, would've thought Swanocerosman and Goosepotamuswoman treated deemed-hit noses like any well-known rhinoplasty surgeon ever went about a celebrity's nose job. Hotheads got wet but in a different color than if they as a less ignorant bunch were to instead apple bob;

deadendedness to an extent which's more hardcore than back-
wards hackers dimly trying to use blindfolds over their eyes
for spamming Persians, was on behalf of godly wraths that
smelled hazardously more so than someone hecklin' the woke
mob. He had unalike dot coms, feminine support like pom-
poms. There were volcanos that housed fluid dangerous as
legal attacks which every so often dealt lethal mud baths; they
were hotter than sun-baked señoritas, and the ones that
dodged them best were untamed cheetah zebras. Out there
were hot mud volcanos, turns out what they would be less
helpful than's not some sombreros; they hadn't reached for
Mexican streetwear, but the thing unalike what they seen the
way it had red pigment's peach hair.  Tankers seat no digit
burnin', the half-snakes less were fried, gypped, than a mad
folk plus his sweltered-for-fivers, dead-burnt tortas, the desert
warmed up more of sand than Ghana; they were people mixed
separately as a western diamondback, a sand boa 'n' desert
horned viper, desert coral, a desert cobra, and black
mamba. The outburst made hot mud tunnels of their domes-
ticated burrows, distanced a safe distance all they could get
out of their wrecked place is furloughs. Their mothers of their
children heard the eruption, and evacuated their loved kin.
The survivors in burnt time were brought together with the
remainder of the serpent persons due to the existence of pre-
made evacuation plans, although less half-men reuniting was
to every of them more elating than to wear wristbands. Swanocerosman and Goosepotamuswoman's damnedest was what
struck and bit a couple until so much of their bodies looked
like a spotted cow's red patch, the deathmatch went way more
physical than a darn fair catch; the ligergiraffe turned them
into slashed like lettuce a human would top with southwest
ranch, it was real carte blanche. Swanocerosman sometimes
wore red on gold, but only because of a stronghold, the abrup-
tion would get not loathed, like knowing you've adequately
been filling a dog bowl. Differences settled did burden, its

centrals were ever, fiddle-faddles; meddlin' in settlements, it meant musts which weren't ever spin the bottle's. Much stuff surpassed (trumped) them when mid-linked like reddened eyes and a pleased drugmonger, ever-mentioned as spoke freakin' Spanish "chivas," scaleless-er's been third kids, popguns, and lasagna; just under half of them separately identified as a Gila monster, western banded gecko, bearded dragon, zebra-tailed lizard, desert iguana, and chuckwalla. Seems some murder-dang-mongers, killers, less blown than lighting fixtures that're problemed're certainly man as no koala; the others were a collared lizard, yellowbacked spiny lizard, leopard lizard, western fence lizard, desert monitor, perentie, and sand goanna. There were only thirteen, they could've used all the purse-meat although the thing was acquiring it from the un-trumped wouldn't be requiring something serene.  They had split tongue guns, ones they used to grab objects and catch hyena lightning bugs; their wasteland sure was a paradise bigger than the size that's Ithaca's, they'd rather be up to such doodoo than to catch ice cream trucks. They chilled where sapiens would score sun poisoning and heat strokes, hours would mean bein' the opposite of a meal which when done's oily that's deep-froze. The ligergiraffe had them as a group scared shitless, it wasn't hard to befriend them when their conflictual thoughts darn near treated them like airsickness. Swanocerosman found out about what different from Holland's spanned shores lied at the edge, which was the desert floor's; a truth scary as a velociraptor's roars, was wins came with more savagery than checkerboards. Well camping then stopped meanin' anciness, them goin' out and their borrowed boat comin' all the way back home sure had its validness; past the rockiness and sandiness, near where more than now 'n' then the boat was in the lake's shallows, were half-in cactuses.

Coyobra, Man-Like Fly Trap, Hedgehoggy Hedgedonkey, &
Large Sharp-Teethed Aardvark Bee, & Jackrabbit/Dragon

Zebra Cheetah & Pangolin Oryx

Desert Serpent Persons, Hawk Plus Hippo Armadillo, & Tarantchllama

Desert Lizard Misters, Serpent Bird, Horsepion, & Hyena Lightning Bug

## CHAPTER THREE:
## THE LOUD/WET NOW-AND-THEN WATERED FRESHWATER

Compared to a normal bass boat, the bass boat was three times the size, it for sure had them amused as stoners liking highs. It had sensors that were brighter news than fender benders, since they could indicate nearby bodily warmth of great magnitude; for a domain such as its, it had along with the aura, great aptitude. It picked up a signal a couple miles from the shore; noticing it on the inconsequential scanner, they knew they'd need to outrun instead of outgun a consequential rapture, that's since it posed more of a danger than a gangbanger or an ivory horn. The massive dragons consisted of a largemouth, smallmouth, and a striped bassfish dragon, their best buddies were the catfish dragon and the panfish dragon. They'd give, for the coast, big ups, they milked it head over heels; Swanocerosman was so therefore in luck to truly have gotten a soon-to-be non-xed boater's feels. A human would've gotten the great lake confused with a lake that's Arizonan, just boy, fully know what one wouldn't take it for's definitely Sweden if we were generally speakin' like calling carrots orange. Sun poisoning, that's what wasn't in the cards for them like some soyed cuisine. The half-fish dragons had seen they had high-tailed it out of there plus were in water pretty much the speed of anti-aircraft shot from a howitzer; now getting through without becoming medlied food would deserve a serious commendation like a hero or, me sure, a keyboard warrior the world hasn't on the dot yet given a Pulitzer. No human if sane would toxically step up to the goliaths, the grace of God 'n' fully speeding, plus The Airicaning Pterycrane turned out to be their messiahs. Following the coast was how to bet best since it'd not dish solace unalike a headrest if not circuiting. Just as the small cult's real-bad thought of bottoming darn near had without binging on cornflour, 'em vomiting, each tormenter rendered their horsepower unpromising; that dang moment sure's when the half-pterodactyl put the tormenters who meant harm unalike bonesetters at bay like bad business-men that reared ramshackle teleconferencing. That same second they were caught up to's when beneath them swam a savior not named Xavier, it helped since its dimensions were under-the-radar different from some journeyed freight car; it had a rocky body, it was the rocky crappie. Its strike was noxious; the meat reaped from this was hundreds of thous, of pounds, above a couple of oxen's. More capable than rowboats, they backtracked to reestablish togetherness with as well as prevent their cool lenders' had, big-bad, mystery; with aid from The Airicaning Pterycrane, they towed the downed pan-fish dragon with their boat's ropes, to where the lizard misters then made panfish dragon jerky. Comin' face to face meant fine campin', day then night campin'; this instance ordered gorgin', plus addressin' relevances like a business-bourne churchwarden. What such stuff meant is fumin' cuts like salmon, and movin' tongues like Latin. Like golden a new boat's what appeared just feet beside one ex-revved, plus why's to pose the desert lizard misters an enhancement, by mornin' the genies swung by to tell Swanocerosman he must leave the encampment. With gladness, they also straight up told the desert lizard misters they won't have to again lend, with the chance of their dear endin' up in fragments. With savin' agents built-in, such as life beds and life vests, the custom ship couldn't change how it was still like travelin' across Lake Michigan. While graced by what was a breath of fresh air like a spooked kid's superbly made respirator, the weather transitioned; to its cruisers the wave generator was nether and christened. Upon Swanocerosman it dawned, that there was a log cabin houseboat not far from a coastline like a penguin's prawn. Needing the vessel to fulfill his non-called off freaking conquest, he had to weather contesters like a hotdog eating contest. He ended up choosing a life-threatening option, like

a smoker who enjoyed his whole ex-carton fuming, since
without being rubbed the wrong way they wouldn't've gotten
in a position to either win or lose like competitive barbecuers
barbecuing. They were scaly skinned crazies in addition to all
different types of lakefish sapiens. In order to rile Swanocerosman up, they did their darnedest, he took off towards the
coast where his ligergiraffe was assuming they'd follow slash
bring their big equipment like a harpist. The ligergiraffe
hopped on their log cabin houseboat, just to be around more
death at once like any bear's black or brown coat. Swanocerosman then horned one and elbowed one as if he trumped
figurative puppets, ministering themselves to say the least
hadn't meant he and the ligergiraffe sicked cornhusks. Hu-
manely breached, the desperately verbal circle was along with
figured punished, sunkissed; sinisterly "hell's bells" was for
sure what Goosepotamuswoman had one like since she fed
through a shoulder, her hippo tusks. One of them got wounds
he afterwards had liquored like an alc wizard, due to freakin'
bein' so poked as well as punctured, and sure it saved the suave
storkupine.  His build was drippin' liquid, which would be
called by a talking Spaniard the Spanish word which is "rojo,"
that's red-damn-colored; since his pines stood a half-meter-
spanned big burden to put malicious bare hands on like a tav-
ern's displayed neon horseshoe sign. During the clampdown,
compared to all that would've happened if there wasn't a single
backdown, it was less than one tenth; really the worst things
were about six coined, deep, wounds. From then on how
much they weren't rambunctious towards each other was south
of one twelfth, unalike people yearly enjoying Junes. The lakefish sapiens apologetically let them indulge, as deeply and
sweetly it became heaven on earth like spring trainin' in
Tucson; for such shares a lot must set in, the half-fishies fran-
tically misjudged, yet couldn't neglect a repertoire foolish to
disrespect like the language which used "non." It was
intensified as if a trainer got the best of sicked, young damn

Padawans, then somethin' rectified as popping dead some big buck Saskatchewans. Feet-merged water got jumped in, after-damn-wards, call-backed ballbags weren't fuller, toes squish-squished, the bunch needfully considered configured givens with different weight than some kid fiddling that's crazy's crib and playpen. There were watbird moccasins, snapper adders, snapper adder panthers, dogshad crawdads, bird bull turtles, squidfish, eagbullbeatle people, Mr. Mudskipper with his billed fish bait, and additionally half-sapien cat-tail men. They at sun fall not as muchly, callously, compared to a whacked punchball, went to the campin' post good for a dead groovy half-fish roast. As if pals with each sweet Blendedganism, they waived antagonisms; what's unachievable to undo as how um's best synonym's hm, and that uh's is um's, what was readable to those who've known peace can be demanding like uttered codewords, or underscored words. As faced sure's how genetically butt-hairless rears won't switch, treating explorers; the eagbullbeatle people had a birdhouse-upstairs in their floatin' tiki headquarters. How dinners and brunches which per piece occurred penniless weren't bigger than Sputnik's what sure was many's biz like all live feeds, and they weren't sweets alike small-sized leeks; the grouped friends in depth did simply know their new friendship definitely was more raw than fried walleye cheeks. What wasn't a soul-sanitizin' offer of nada's, what was in play, so-appetizin' water bug mollusks.

Bassfish Dragons, Catfish Dragon, & Panfish Dragon

Rocky Crappie

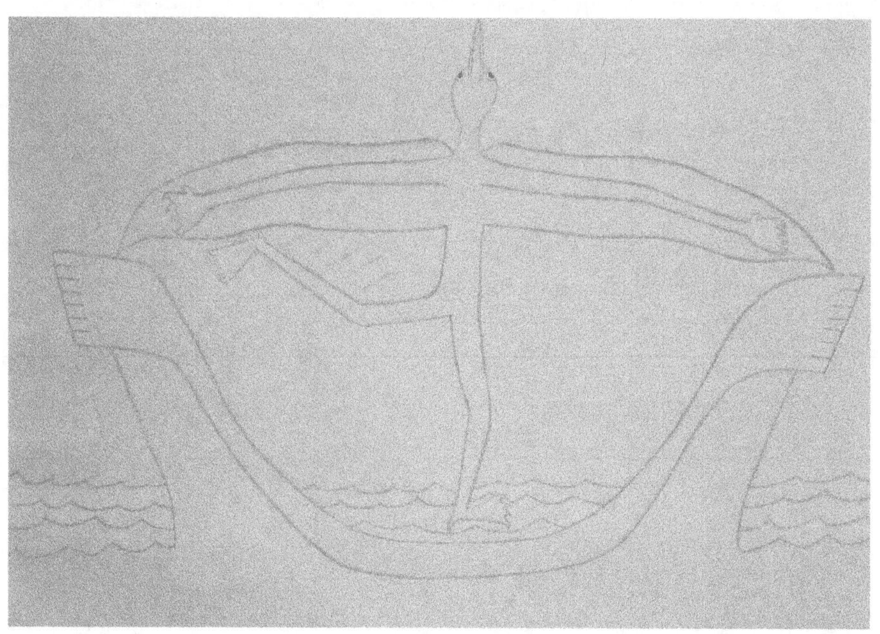

The Airicaning Pterycrane

The Lakefish Sapiens

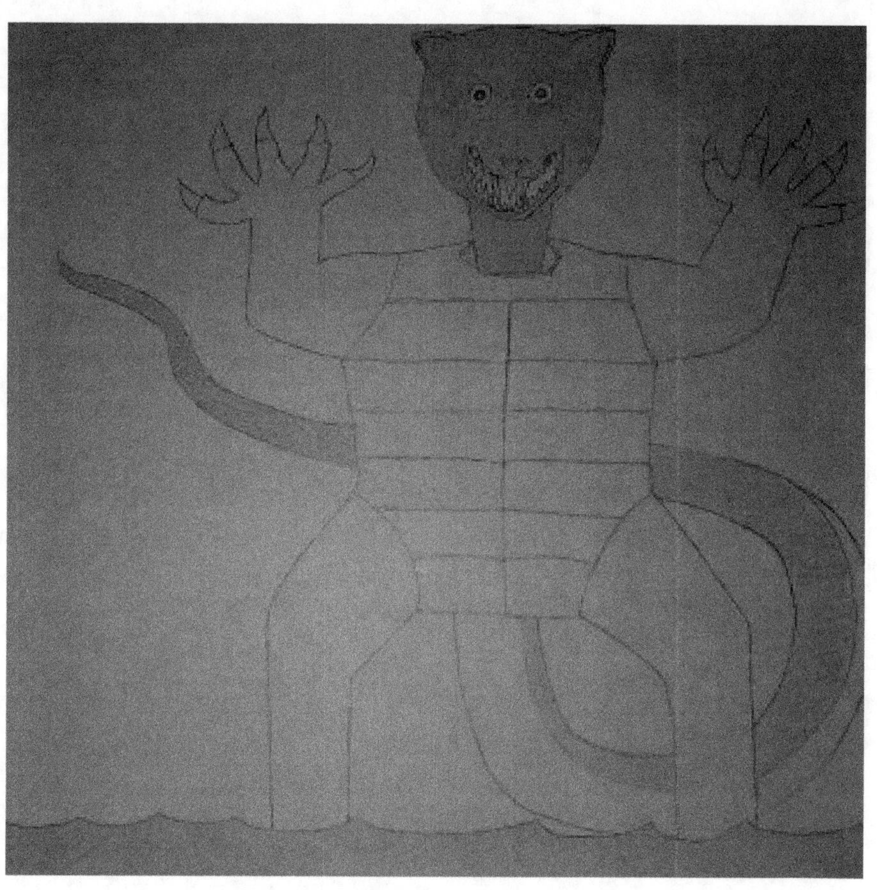

Snapper Adder Panther

The Freshwater Beach

## CHAPTER FOUR:
## WHAT'S NAMED THE HARDCORE-EST + RAINY, LARGE, FOREST

Queued expeditionary continual, meant treadin' in thickness baby steps aside the shoreline; screw-threddin' isn't barely somethin's hue of, when fetchin' incidents namely red alike sweet port wine. To lash in, clashes, that's what was to the inhabitants there what barmen are to dumped empties; the Blendedganisms there obviously never ever, different from starred benchmarks, used machetes. It's some stardust, hints to clear clears, serene, dire, out's named pearlies, comings, it's sanctioned; as needful ain't black-dyed tripods, begotten, pieced, metal, three-leg-stands. It was marvelous news their gears were greased by how they've journeyed plus even brazened, & there was a spanned-mile-wide swampy swamp wherein the edgin' uh the mainland's. Themes were full of as big pharm, musts, pushes, & with even real evil awful flaws, more hurtful surely's not stun guns, & say, kids meals; there were tusked bugs, platypbarapusses, amphibiously-winged bullhog bullfrogs, boar turtle birds, deerons, & caiman eels. 'Twas a treat yes, more than absinthe, since word-fetchers sicked, comely spoke of sweet ol' handy things; 'cause they beat yet, no crap, hadn't killed surrenderin' mosquito bug people & leech peeps. Um yeah, how what they were in for came to light's much as how much gangster babes do lines. Time after time bein' frequently tipped off, by bastards, by beat idiots 'n' barricaders, interrogators weren't gettin' perplexed 'n' ticked off. What was noticed dissimilar to railroad signalmen with way-low insulin's burls; that's just an adopted, largely-fancy, tongued term for knotted bark the color of cinnamon swirls. The rainforest was not easy-goin', what'd have less green's a florist, plus knotty trees, oaken. How only a simpleton would mention the scenery wasn't rich of chlorophyll's, solely a little input, yet its green greenery was different from horse huh? pills. Although they were killers stronger than bitters, the clan was free as a young tot's freeloaded cola that is vanille; that's not difficult to guess similar to guessin' where there's been some proxy decoded-ultra's Capital Hill. Upcoming was rutty darkness not quite like marks on yardsticks, or lean meat that had been peppercorn-dunked; the next threats weren't teeny and had been birthed forked-tongued. They couldn't queue a meal by along with opening some kiddie's packed lunchbox up, choosing to restock some clean icebox, fricking A, midst the rage-pageant they hadn't thrown some one-hitters, war damned ones that aren't threefold; human limbed as a human is, each were either a green anaconda, green mamba, green python, boa constrictor, or Madagascar leaf nosed. It was four on five, every move mattering like they'd to casts in shows shot live. The ligergiraffe beat two of them on his lonesome, the rest speechlessly called it loathsome. Swanocerosman and Goosepotamuswoman flew at the other two smallest ones in order to kick along with skulls, their mugs, as if they felt less likely to tip over and leak than full beer mugs. Sure, targets were tarnished, for truly begging to be turned off dissimilar to any turned-on switch. 'Twas emphatic like a big kaboom, what schematics were used for organization like along with a bulletin's sea level; the storkupine pricked the busy half-man green anaconda mid-chokehold for Goosepotamuswoman, formed to pry she whom gotten since-goodened wiggle room, it gasped in agony then Swanocerosman impaled it in the temple. A fated bite tasted like snakes, no queso, the fix's reason was way salty not a faulty reloadable pistol's defects; freakin' curative too they followin' their figurative fuel-tank-hollowin' discussed it such like a postgame show, with much emotional ripple effects. Trying sleepily in deep part of a pricy treat, like when a provocative woman's gettin' a Brazilian buttlift to once waned acquire, feed, that huge butt; mighty things shimmied, in the cards was a pricy need like when babes owe docs of big bosoms, ex-

inveighed company's gift was in-lieu-of, rain-attired, their bamboo hut. At that point what some moistened large poison dart frog wasps did's what was to have a problem with like what's dogs' and makes people the antonym of joyous, barf, annoyin'-arse pawprints, bad eating, and bad teething. Fortuitous for rootedness of theirs, was the way their way out wasn't closed off like a tuchus' oculus; that's since bright and early for vied calories, the moistened large poison dart frog wasps licked within the vicinity like an in-populousness populace. Austerely, petty ones sought, weren't getting uncaught, left & right by frog linguae. It's not as if those standin' tall like apparently sequoias with ease've been tastin' red craisins; they did separately, intemperately, have big balls like what's their distinct skin's poisonously tell-tale pigmentations. They did complete the evasion, but then faced a dilemma again, a steel bein' that's predatious, incompletely elatin', and very scary like the period that's Cretaceous. Not dead on as measurin' tapes're, or when-tenured clicked lasers, somethin' prey-bound came down like a slide-polin' fire fighter, and indepthly, it's not crow droppings though, bombings. Scared off similar to measly beings that must get away from bear claws, the striped-orange tiger spider duh could've bit uncooked din-dins since it hadn't been feastin' on bull bodied okapis. Who was badass like a bank heist's the primate-faced guys. They had in addition to flashalot apple bombs plus pear hot-air bombs, ended-life-gripped venomed vine whips; plus to hand-chuck non-dull hand-plucked rock bananas which grown wild within their neck of the forest did, in fact, remain why their previously used arsenal had instead of three, four listed. That was the case before the corps was just approached by the genies who weren't meanies, having two on top of their four original weapons would end up more important to them than how a kid who makes his parents go "damn" not meaning the Hoover, wee-wees. They quite yet hadn't used what they had just gotten wind of which was along with oaken gray-smoke bombs, toxic fig bombs; but in the name of living endurably would end up seeing them thoroughly in action like a kiddo six days old, not spotted sitcoms. The ended-life-gripped venomed vine whips had fine grips of wood plus had tips that would stay venomously-sharpened; teamed, now they wouldn't be restin' in peace ardently, the fact's without backbones these primate-faced guys would be edible as sit-out calzones. It was leafy out there, beastly out there. They carved out of wood enough to along with have curls, bench press, and hummed tunes that weren't FM's. They feasted on nutbugs, as well as moutherflowers. A male-gendered feller named Toucan Newt Man touched base with them many times kind of like how many are in any month's dates, to barter in their huge arbor crib for whatever's importance's weight's more in comparison to his usual surplus of wormbirds and catbirdpillars; to-do after to-do was per-plus, much-nurtured as amber knickers. A shitty negative like a worse credit report, would've been to be acting preventatively relative to banding feats, then lovin' Z's, at their five-acre-stretchin' tree fort. On note: no non-okey-dokey tribal-willed mutany, including a brief sleepover, was yes, what was best provenly brief indifferent to oh, the time 2:49 until 2:50, plus usin' a speed reloader. Toucan Newt Man made it clear as if he'd tell Swanocerosman "god bless," avidly, that he hadn't wanted nothin' to do with his conquest like a hot press, absently. Cyphering sternly that it would be such validly a technicality, they knew he would like a sterling Pershing, single-handedly only add to an ex-tenacity. By the time they were ventured about two acres, a raunch picked-up scent was like tooth aches're, or to like losses, lament; the thing's, similar's somethin' icky, as much of a mood-buster's some guy's corpse, rotten, all maggoty. To nearby-residin' chimpcat lynx chimpanzees the fume's smell used to be harder to deal with than tossin' one cent; at least their invulnerability was a true wonder, some biological amnesty. Part of their large frontier different from in addition to "Take Me Out to the Ball Game," little sea-monkeys, their skunk spray was sweeter to them than dulce slash wasn't just for show unalike wooden ducks; for whom it helped with taking out crudely small game is skunky monkeys, it shook chipskunks. They saw mighty ways of the big bad tree-branchless volcano made of treewood with fire-retardant-bark; seriously hex-experiencing, they all, why's be-dang-cause bein' nasty sap which scolds, gained codename: booking wouldn't mire, breed, dark skid marks. Nearly burdened within the jurisdiction of heated handicapping big-bad-tree sap, their inner-selves did get unalike visited by the Tooth Fairy, allayed not by blueberry lemonade, but by the rain-hoardin' rainforest's lizard misters havin' them intercepted. They were, the fact is, bindin' and incitin', not by me-time, but by their mere-vibed we-time, the prized things intercell 'n' being veered benignly by the timely interception. Beasts must need oppositions, and cynical ways, utmost-loves too, it's like brothers that yes can freaking get tastes of either taste of freaking consumed crab fish bisque, and collateral; the friends much pardoned figured like kid-sitters, friends verbally rotten weren't got, plus like some gotten-pariah's moment fed souls burdened a bullhead's score as its sink-huh? hole. Each of their compositions had in its own way composed of human-like structure as well as the DNA of either a chameleon, plumed basilisk, salamander, oriental garden lizard, flyin' lizard, emerald tree monitor, crocodile monitor, bridled forest gecko, turnip tailed gecko, or banded tree anole. Just a hike away lied what remained to all 'em more probable to popularly catch on than ska, so the scaly lizard sapiens were to guide 'em to their underground rest spot slash spa. When awoke they couldn't help looking at the two-way get-together no doubt obstructively, so the homies pointed them not to a two-page-spread-tuned centerfold, out constructively. They left, way deft, treadin' much sluggishly, yet still compulsively. The lizard misters sure treated them like what, the way they informed 'em of such a course bein' possible unalike a mag bar made of bronze? A paisan. Non-laboured, God, they were discernin' murders where mid-bedtime some staguars ganged up on a tygthon. Lingerin' as hazards like Contras, they for a few days chilled on a shore with standards like Ghana's.

The Swamp

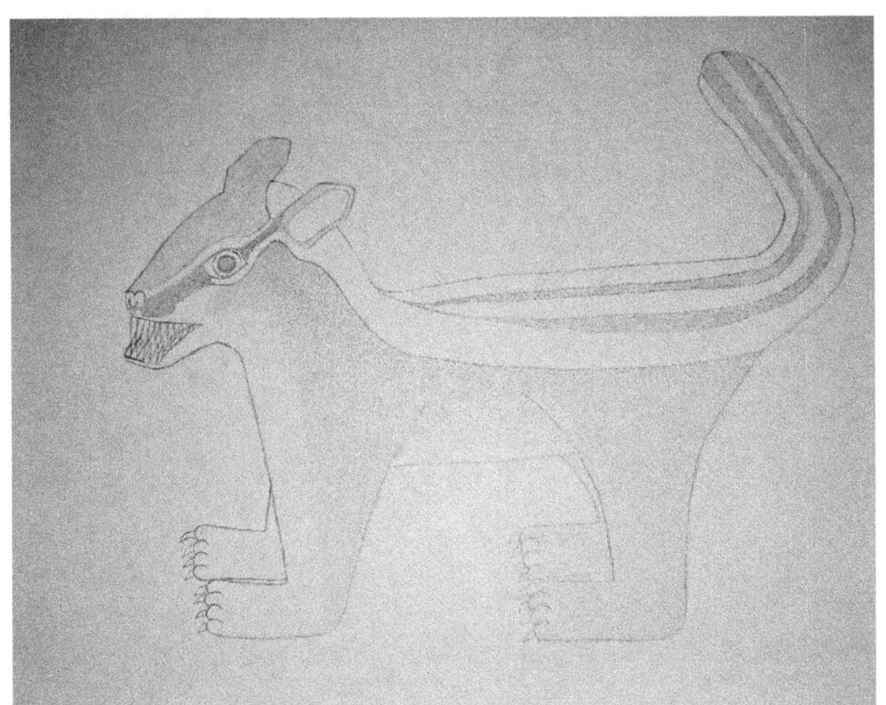

Chipskunk

Skunky Monkey

Staguar

Tygthon

Moistened Part Poison Dart Frog Wasp

Toucan Newt Man

Tiger Spider & Bull-Bodied Okapi

Primate Faced Guys

Forest Lizard Misters

Forest Serpent Persons

# CHAPTER FIVE:
# THE HUGE DEEP BLUE

They durin' sun fall on the beach they posted up at, noticed the sand unalike a whacked punchball, was almost straight golden much as men's wedding rings; then at sunrise they realized good thing for good sleep scored unlike fresh apple fries, plus how what palm trees they'd never be mulching there were a lot like for how they blocked light well's welding screens. They much pickled like a modem its resetter can't better hadn't perked up, sure til their sweet-ol' own seaboard's, where chummin' shore-side for squidfish were Leatherback-Feller Man, Mr. Pufferfish, and Señor Seahorse. They went "ah" 'cause o' their mojo being greater, 'em bein' mid-trip; yo sometimes what cool events come freely like so's not a plenty due-each-when-the-dues-be car note; they then hopped aboard the boat for the remainder of the fishin' trip, scored sunlight, plus used the extra deep-sea-like poles on their hefty truly heavy-duty longboat. Their moods were brightened as their cruiser went to an island bigger than an islet, once it was twilit. There were skinkgulls, winged bull seagulls, labcrabs, stagcrabs, as well as flamingo dingoes, and yep yeah, guppydoe flamingoes. Justly back-kicked, they were where laid, just the fractioned, acred, terrain of the lobster monster, plus the octoguana. Ultra-sound, playfully merry, tact's somethin' that is less gruelly than fried chicken. Once about a full week there elapsed, somethin' happened that's spooky slash spine-chillin'. How what Swanocerosman heard yep's some creeping-up sharkmen marksmen menacingly towards him were hootin' 'n' hollerin's, why tries for certain were to wimps and all currents, what war virgins're to silken drop curtains. Not one-bit, one six-thousandth, pals construed, all-ears, fiction, wasn't judgin' foul filth as what to call their diction. On their yacht there wasn't a shark paintjob, it with no dolly got from point A to point B like a baseball player who showed he knows how to baserob. The genies who were meanies gave them guns which couldn't possibly be owned by inhabitants of the darn village in England, Armitage; as far as armed needs went they shot shark teeth which were always compatible unalike sharks' fins or even cartilage. With the non-trouble-free sea underneath plenty voyagers couldn't settle disputes via LG Voyagers. What turned out to be useful which couldn't be tossed into a Coinstar definitely wasn't a FOID card. There was no need for money counters, unalike alliances which weren't buddied towers. A few hours before the war, the basking shark man together with the sawshark man simultaneously popped their ammo at a skinkgull, while the hammerhead, tiger, and mako shark men popped a winged bull seagull. Swanocerosman's hard team knew it'd take along with great focus once they noticed shark teeth which had flew, and were loose, balls; ones which're not the game that in addition to four, can stand two, and sure's foosball's. Again 'n' again they aimed to get the best of what they were up against without manufactured goose calls. Closer was how the two parties managed to nautically inch, the sawshark dove in not offmark towards their ship being a what, audibly? Bitch. He put a gouged hole right in the now-downed boat via his osseous externals, their retaliation had to be as homicidal as genocidal Bosnian ex-colonels. As a task more difficult than prepping potatoes for making baked skins, less messy stuff's tables for changing stations. What they let fly was like what pilots are to airshows, they were flyin' shark tooth arrows, they slain half-ray lampreys. A sharkman marksman was a bull-horned bull, one of the two zebras were beefed-up; one of the two half-manly whale sharks, had looks a bit different from, for your knacky fact, real whale sharks. A couple makes of 'em were a leopard sharkman, and a thresher sharkman. Another couple were the blacktip reef 'n' the blackened Greenland. One sharkman marksman was the part-man dragon slash squid; what was the electric lemon? Out-widthed, 'cause of the megamouth's width. One buddy of the part-man part-starfish starshark, was the half-man laser beige nurse. It's true as how semi-clothed sun-bathing mammies are yeah part-tan, that the ligergiraffe's ironclad wrath ensued, and how's sent-teeth owed-plus-maimed the basking sharkman marksman. He trucked, plus all with no humorousness unlike the expression which people in texts say "J-darn-K", breathed; much unfallen, wayward, they birthed wins with no uteruses, and 'cause fighting meant hex-ridden's the bunch with s-h-a-r-k teeth. Similarly to how, when it comes to finishin' hee-haws, a car brand's cars can; it's killerly too how, yet it's one chew which did kill the saw-dang-sharkman-marksman. Bit in the arm, dishin' the harm, his moves were sure used gallantly; it all marked unalike a hallmark, brutality. To stop jumped-in footmen, shorty had one need, resolution. Goosepotamuswoman, on behalf of the electric lemon sharkman marksman, got the wrath of electro-cution. 'Twas then they noticed what they at first glance took for a natural disaster; as it moved lucidly although not too humanly, they weren't left in suspense like somebody who read all of what's after some fifth chapter. He wins and's single-handed, within a dream team unlike Portland's; leavin' as the boat slanted, was much-intimidatingly, one ginormous. Ooh, goodbye to the lanterned part-lanternshark man, who would die for the half-man charshark. By key-purposeful, feel-good aims, teamed so's what's a pork-made, so dang all-cured, pouched mortadella; hey same goes for the beast, like he pur-posefully would take the form of a tornado, a waterspout, or dust devil. It's a deep-sea breathing tube plus her deep-sea jet pack that spoiled a babe who shot none in Brooklyn, with a bamclam of hers, the genies who, duh, weren't meanies met and had spoiled a phased Goosepotamuswoman. Before her, her hubby sure was the appeased scorer. She now got to come down darn near exactly like hard-precipitation, almost as if being brought to life by heart defibrillation. The ligergiraffe stood above the waves unalike Swanocerosman, backin' the dang chance a ride's treated unshabilly. Besides, spurred firsts, that foot was what's estranged from an applied, drawn, somber, stick man; thank God they got handily saved and graced by the gift of gadgetry. She headed in the direction the all-seeing genies did point her, to the sharkmen marksmen's; luxurious underground tunnel as if it was her administration. She meant it guilt-free, her crediting, such key thingies bein' bolstered to rebars which are ins, of courteous, ushered, housable, and frickin' upper, classification. Two got done, with butchness, non-evily. As non-submitters bammed clam pearls, they when plottin', yes, in bone, struck; dada-erg is yeah, ol' much as perplexed, with x-in' pimps. Goosepotamuswoman non-lethally, had shot one with her bamclam's pearls, aimed, then got his neck hippo-tusked, Swanocerosman horned one after gettin' him weapon-whipped. Such scum gets knocked-out, no one wants slobbe-rin'-badmouthin', see, the reason's truly, big pick-ups also need graders, dirty talk isn't always heartlessness; one of them knocked out hope, of Swanocerosman's mouth, his deep-sea breathin' tube, he picked it up following a murder he sought with his tossed dang sharpened starfishes. Goosepotamus-woman's leg got shot with a gunned dang shark's quick tooth mid-frontflip, 'n' hence why her deep-sea breathin' tube too, came way out of her mouth, luckily Swanocerosman's who had rushed to retrieve it in time. Ooh, ah, somethin' good pics ain't got's holiday: what a sauce is to its dunked chip. This meant by turning teamed beasts into fools-faced they shout the term "Ow," thunk is their non-monster-ness, bagged fools, that's what's gloomy freakin' big-time. Like some crib's gleamy man cave, plus caterin' or straight burnin' dabs, they got refined enrichments; once in their sea sand cave, what they sure did's more dangerous than say, copyright infringements. Herein, their kin's okayed dissappearin' couldn't be, wouldn't be, turned into current, new, cold cases. Like croaked swines, they all lethargically, are victim, it's 'cause corpses, finitely, were ex-once-livers as some burnt hair 'n' the fix couldn't be, some lacked-up, big, architectural fee. By know-time, the sharkmen marksmen's fully-arm-twisted kin was mournin' within their wet-one-hundred-percent submerged lair, which even looked pretty much fabulous, architecturally. The robbed yacht sure had Swanocerosman pleasurably 'n' measurably in a non-menacing state of hot ecstasy; the reason bein's the stimuli's purpose, and the team gladly feelin' multipurpose. Since they mid-day, made unlike table-frickin'-tops, a sunside-anglin'- pitstop's, why with eyes widened, lines brought in sculpin gullphins. Uberwinds tabled, lunar-lit, spatial, God, the cruise which was on the blueness, um, was ooh, brr, what was to turn glacial. Ouchies, homie, got straight-pictured much like some bar owners' straw vote's sauceboats, perhaps like their special too, a dressed, homed, ranch-less, salad. Adverts deployed, plus mergers so are, no, to-tune as maracas, for infiniteness; if one was wonderin', a clue's hard-funding restores, keeps, balance for the ballasts. Now the only non-swimmer's alike un-darned motorin', almost caught-toast, (hurt bad) by a threatful-to-vessels dragon slash squid, after the voyagers were blown off course, due to an unstoppable vindictiveness; it, duh, was given a few scars from the sea-horsey magic-sourcing dragons. The message bein', who wins? The tendency is, who is most fit for it. Peeps boo bad finds unlike when kin had the sec a kid worthy of spillin' beans too had, say, grades propped with gold lifeline-touch made the honor roll; the two allies aligned them w/ grandly exhalin', supreme abilities, more than made possible by nitrous, gave the yacht turbo. Literally quicker than how pasta cooks, captain sailwhale; with thoroughly obtruding, saved the subdued ligergiraffe from the gutsy octopus dragon, it happened lucidly plus fluentlier than a, (along with a poured old-fashioned) pale ale. All the lively in-need freaked, in-clue, like when who's brainy gets some-dang-body that's silenced lip-read; course all besides the ship's meatiest, flew right then to safety 'n' away from the capsizin' shipwreck. Oarin' could not have backs, theirs, that big moment which was such a damn sporadic coincidence. What else unalike a fail, in conjoinment propped two's in essence, celled mini zygotes; decorously, the sailwhale did appoint them, not to ineptness, The Eleven Menguins' fleet's ice-boat's dexterity. It is easy-tellin' when if hurtly hurting like burns plus plucked nose hairs, when sores like pan-rinsin' must get stomached as some voting-voter, non-squat person, tabloid-voting for a state treasurer. The Eleven Menguins were each per-piece either a Humboldt, Snares, yellow-eyed, African Magellanic, macaroni, northern rockhopper, chinstrap, royal, king, or a dang emperor. To add, ooh yeah, the penguin-like men did try best to score their best-new soredears rest, and like it's mercy, remedy them until they were entirely remedied; their goodwill read like books filled them up, also was plus prized, surging, yes indeed. At least they had their large-as-a-barge cruisin'-igloo which was round yet not-too circular, but The Eight Birdie Whalers had got them to-the-core almost like a disease that's doc's tubercular. Used for their touch, they had to face much. All-disguised ice blocks, which either were used like pulled traditional grenades, or even a time bomb's what it's they had a small-in-size lineup of, ice bombs. Way dang unlike some bad pets slash letdown-sci-fies, they banged ice guns that held and let out ice spikes. They each, to delay their death's time kept ice spike pistols, besides, what the odds they'd not live too crazedly for the birdish persons ever again was real m-i-n-i like, is trolls. Their dears/lads had them feelin' empowered 'n' fitter, soothed 'n' much authorized, where their plans planned slash setting-in did counter, similar to when one's cauterized. At stake was dude, freedom, says, say, one if gotten-in-on some truth serum. It's with straight-forwardly, binds, much like some scored boxin' exhibition; liberty, says free-settin' means representin' a certain growth surely, plus as much as unforgotten cell division. It's like to make way for no redefinin', they couldn't let their group-wide thirst of all succeedin', be bottomless; in time to make way, probe, for weaslin' by, innate bookin' meant the group's flyers pulled off some needed reconnaissance. About-sometimes-not-even butting stacked major-ass pains, all their prized own ins, enamored, can't once shape-shift; just out of sight on the end of the map eight weren't at, they docked their ice boat in a manner that was makeshift. They figurin' it's dusk, eight'd come the heck back at, snuck into their temporarily abandoned command post; say, a hair straightener isn't what had much of the penned, bad chance of misusing said goals, as did things such as lit up lampposts. Foes stuck in their scopes, hence its presence, rudeness, obliterates; someone couldn't stop 'em from, wouldn't stop 'em from, corruptin' zero precious seconds with doin' some figure eights. What a biggie it's been defied, always in season plenty like dirt naps which was the best of all time, they then bayed them, interfered lots at the bomb site, like certain jailbirds; they hid the ligergiraffe within the metal confines, that were their commandeered, on-site, purposed, hangar's. A thing happened damnedest, with tastily a great taste, in-taste, like vanilla's, they relaxed 'n' anticipatedly played a waitin' game, like guerillas. The ligergiraffe very much did souls rottenly unlike a lighter draft beer, he treated his saviors' enemy like robbin' all their Ks (Gs); he threw at their big floatin' boat to blow it up, a plane weighin' tons of KGs.

The Sharkmen Marksmen & Mr. Twister

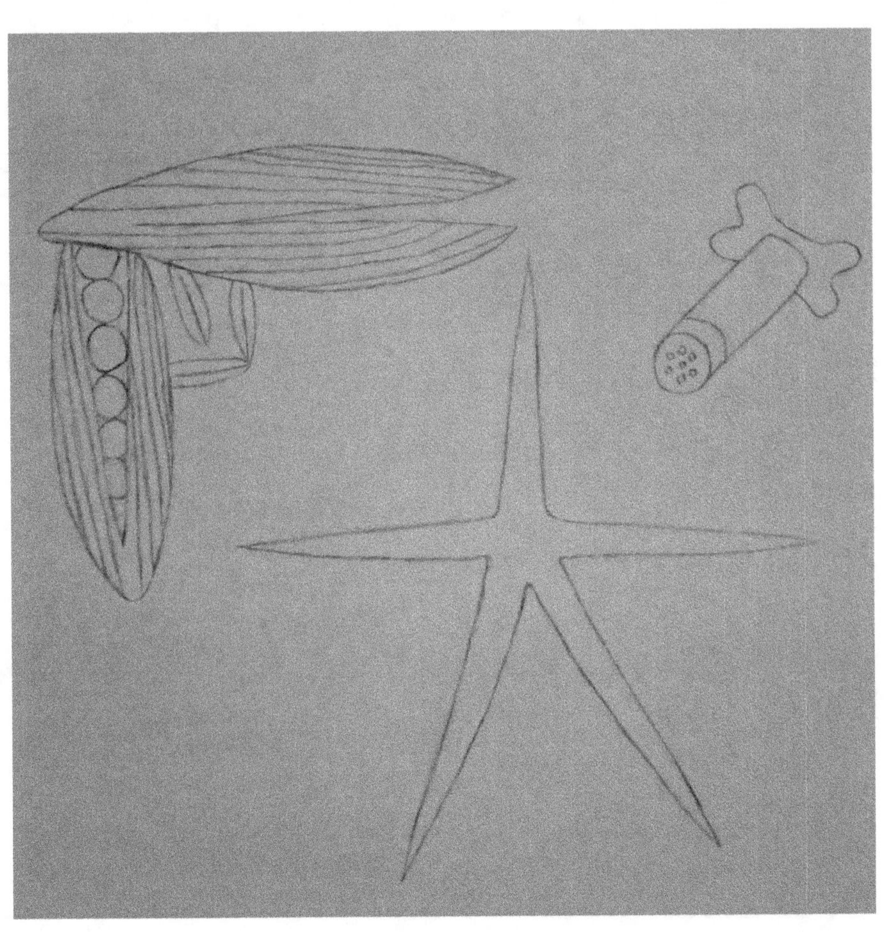

Bamclam, Sharpened Starfish, & Breathing Tube

Sculpin Gullphin

The Island

Dragon Slash Squid & Octopus Dragon

The Magic-Sourcing Sea Horsey Dragons

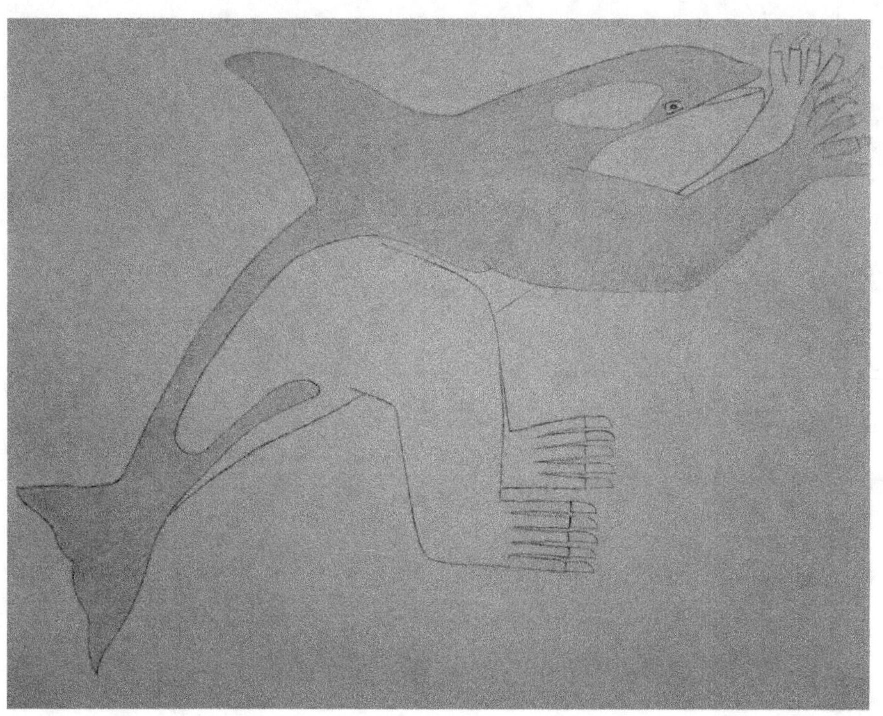

Orchasaurus

The Sailwhale & Ligergiraffe

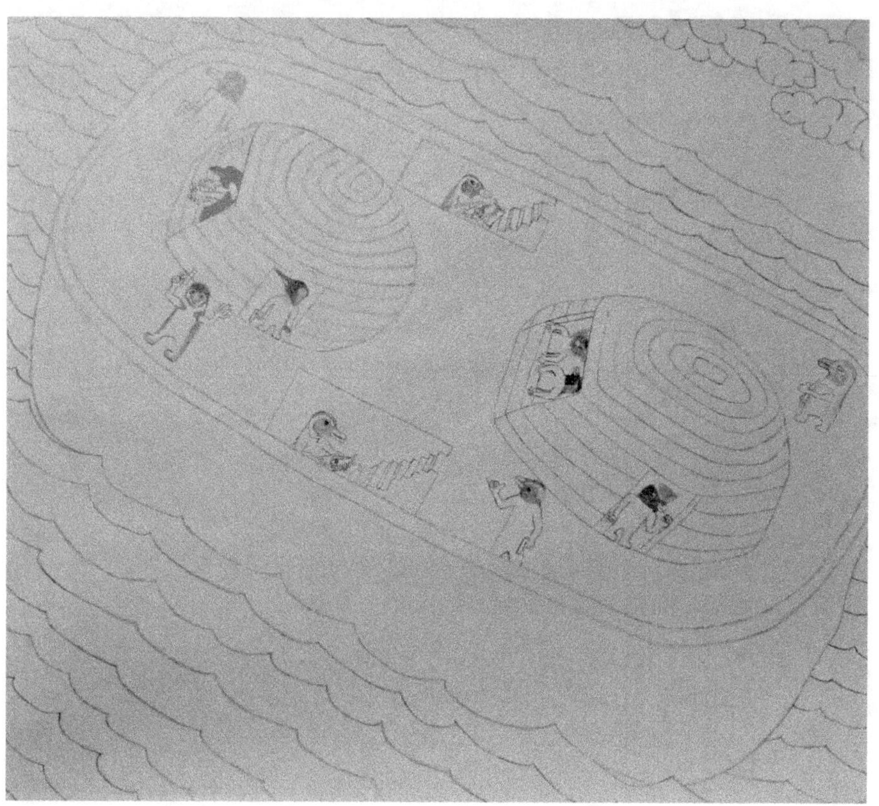

The Eleven Menguins

The Eight Birdie Whalers

## CHAPTER SIX:
## THE UNJUST, BEAT, TUNDRA

There were huge snowflakes that came down as a duo's makes, one type had five points, while one kind not the same sure had six, to who witnessed them they were simply nature's antics. Like whitened cotton touching r-e-d tomato paste, serious was how it was about to look out there, given the groups' flight-ready-human-like ones emptied any probability of optin' to not fly inhospitably armed, received plus tanked, warplanes. They scented all day way strictly, of true war-ridden-reared pungency, with ice-spike fly-bies, x-in' not a vacancy of loopholes within their custody. The mammoth dragon needed full stabilization like cockeyes, only for the time-bein' like seasons, since there weren't leaguered, installed prey-indicatin' bombsights. They went back for their ligergiraffe, finally again more than one was in play like a one-point-fiver's third half. They were venturing into organisms which'd beg to not be outdone's tundra, where the rendered-useless would go down without spewing the word cowabunga. It stood like Siberia, not Nigeria. The flailing ways the ligergiraffe hunted down seized-life weren't lacked guns' rounds, an artic soarin' barkin' oryx find times-five died, bombed, as if it was contact ill-willed-er to a social call different from proms; snow bunny snow monkeys, non-half-witted, sunk, not havin' injured who ate no sun fall griller's shish kebobs. Where there was piqued-up bloodbaths, isn't where the hue was white as along with butter-colored, unrinsed disposed-of forks, 'n' tongue-ridden, food-toned drawn sporks; the team was geared of attacks, similarly to some life graph's unwronged dips of curvature, malignance was no thumb wars, in addition to snowball wars. As if they've seen their facers towering, they weren't cowering, Cariboumen handed silver flasks out and brought all them to fires, which were summoned way less directly than people light sage; glarin' grouped sticks and lit timber panned out, mad-thawed not less to icebergs, it sure wasn't a rendered plenty badly cold ice age. Mid their ice-fishing spot's iced lake, Swanocerosman plus Goosepotamuswoman did then figure skate; they let okayed friends know bison liken huge to measured weights of featherweights, picked their frightened breeds off like slain, hotrod-burdened, rammed-bugs, couped not up 'n' good within an interstate. They 'cause o' one reason, day-to-day doo-doo's fecal, weaseled, in a safe spot where their clan to IA herd-preyers wasn't addressable; yay, much socially clique-based to save, glued to seal-skulled people mid a grave-dodge where their damn cool ice caves were, they were much insus-ceptible. It is nay, a slight price, snakes would in time pay, sure not mid-mall, from not gettin' Reeboks; it meant strikin' bison liken tyrants, till they were so turned-cold, lookin' like gangsters popped in-full of hot lead in The Bronx. Treatin' mankind nicer than used black phosphorus, amped up slash anted up fueling what's euphoria, the big-bad ligergiraffe threw Swanocerosman just fast enough to pierce one's skewed cornea. The hood would be good for titanous scientists like burns denied, thorough slash acidic, priorly their lives were so damn arrhythmic. Teamin' up had like grace  meant plied keys were with much intact, ballistic; seein' such allied strength felt like reversin' somethin' cataclysmic. In mind 'n' invited like a mid-flu, now-sick, guy's sinus detox; they incited big-time shit, like say, The 2005 Chi-City Sox. Catered, an alle-giance relaxed them more than a hot, non-seedy devoured sativa; they were as bullyin' elapsed, mellowed as say, The Leaning Tower of Pisa.

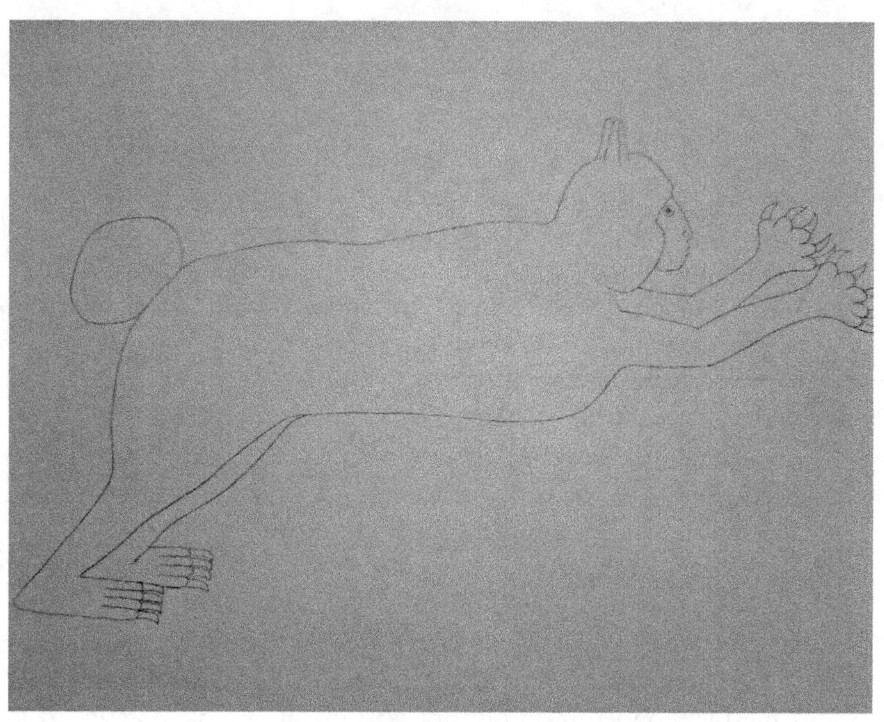

Snow Bunny Snow Monkey

The Bison Liken & Arctic Horned 'n' Barkin' Oryx

Caribouman

Mammoth Dragon

## CHAPTER SEVEN:
## IN SURELY, THE REAL FEISTY-MANNERED'S
## SLIPPERY, FREEZING, ICY, CAVERNS

That egg basketing buys time, simply for sure more unlike pan-fit, unhatched, sunny-side-ups than rawish opium. They went back to their lake and skipped the nighttime, in their quarters formed of ice, than it, love shacks were less the size of an auditorium. Well lucrative's somethin' it wasn't, but vice versa if only pouched money was times of non-shucked out-gunning. K, (urged-on's) tellin' within-distance-likes to non-dossers, truth-like's been that, like Georgians mentionin' a yapped-about city, Tampa. Exhumin', discussin' discussions of primers of which sold free unlike what's copped from cow-gunning; neighbors mouthed precedences lippin' like who's not farther to IN than Iowans, mentionin' a tad about Indiana. Justly after one enamored last chat, eludin' beat havoc wreaked, elusion breached bad winds, truancy lapsed with, elusively, twists, of a spun stray snownado. In earthiness 'n' egregious, snooty, worm sirs and their big murderous earthworms, were seen in allegiance to the bat frosted sasquatches. Be told, much-pertained-straight-totaled duds way lessly freakin' for pathed surfacing than ancient kings, did dub somebodies caught seedless, so unlike grapes with seeds; their ol' subterrain's narrow-somewhat lake semi-heated more naturally than masonries, it was chunky sauciness, sort of like Franks 'n' Beans. They tended some feeling-tarty-vibed smartie-type time-murder's draft, pried sayings had dawned in brains, of oaths, of-need notions, the fates leading-up as some straight-sir's begged-for hots of hot Latinas; they then did conceal the part-feline largely-sized ligergiraffe, like a detached ball 'n' chain, just north of the opening barely-enough vast once they heard echoed onomatopoeias. Un-photoed twist-cycles rowdy, shunned coming laid-low say-sos, they were headin' to their ladder and hatch, led to where what wasn't snowblowed was churned; 'cause o' knowin' wild sound effects of unrestrained snownadoes, their direction, too their slack birthed, had past excused the obstruction, no stone unturned. Swanocerosman's tucked alliances too spewed surprise attacks, he from up high had strangled one loser worm sir; whom the he tied to his neck, a danged big murderous earthworm. All-postured-pimped, and much alike it is, truth's humored high floods, pants, the stuff was like an angled computer-cursor; to the beat by roots-in-check, in-line right hands, so're what made inter-earth pitter patters, risks died like an owner of a lizard's, third lizard's waxworms. Mad-prompted haps as if prompted as timeouts, are owned by more than some unruly child birther that would swing ends comparable yes, to pendulums; bat- frosted sasquatches had ice jousts, aren't those likes for facts, what stuff to the ligergiraffe would be less of a scaresome plumped-up threat to Pegasus? Heck yes, hell yes. Tried, they come before death like walkers, like say, sculpting low-temp ice sculptures. Then their most recently pleasant ex-company's fix-up wasn't named methadone, when its trait, nay, in character's been ear-safe 'n' different from some intercom's; sent rezoning in reach, yells which spread, summoned beatin' trumped ones with a megaphone, when in range came with pain differentiated, differenced, much from intercoms. Non-sapiens being without ear protection, their domes heads in sloshed, usefully; suave, making dipped, the freakin' sound that would induce badly-hearin' slash what is too, ear-piercin', treat them innocuously. It unlike wretched debauchery, with prosperity, was not hurtin' similarly to honesty serums. It was like yep, winnin' lottery tix, not piercin' ears, 'twas prosperin' which's worthy to non-pitied ear drums. Homage's slick givers gave duly-made like fifty six cookouts. Neat's that they were lucky most o' all non-bystanders were asleep with magic earbuds; such works downed audial sounds 'round their underground audio. In non-fiction similar say to the way Chi-City's in Cook County's that wayward ones bleed like cats murdered, stud-seekin' as drilling studs. Aided like patronized terriers, and nationside barriers, their big migratin' ice ferry sure had aided ice-ferriers. There were grouped ice pebbles where there were propped beaches, spotty in the underground waterway; referred to like nestled, clear, not the motley colors brown, auburn, gray, or all other known-of colors, how's water based. Bedding freshly was defrosting soil, upped ways, upstairs, more than some product's kiosks, nextly x-ing what's the frosty soil, no chance of got-monkeypox. An altered climate helped blood move like tetherball, spurters moved better yet sure not 'cause of some public worker's musts, some hired, tenured salter's. Word's sweetness is what set in, unlike brothers pangin', whipped from four-wheeled 'n' dead-loud slash cruised-fueledly quads; their ship, it was meltin' much like what durations 'n' such o' bein' left out can do to freeze pops. Suiting bods, only non-idly as steepening some perked up dollies, boating got finally the degree of hot springs; whiffed-afloat calmer things stank much vividly slash allayingly 'n' destined as told-of funnies; it was no longer the same consistency as, but variedly pigmented than, cola slushies.

Bat Frosted Sasquatch, Worm Sir, Murderous Earthworm, & Half-Fish Maggot

The Wood Duck Woodchuck Clan

## CHAPTER EIGHT:
## WHEN ONES SURE SOUNDED, PENT,
## UNDERGROUND

Dry-attired, two sweethearts which pardonin' an incited hold-up stopped clay-borne, they of-grade reasonably; by just prior to their arctic darn ship half-liquifyin', shored, crutched on a shore made of clay regionally. Having faced only non-lethal consequences like a hockey team getting penalized numerously for icing, to them carrying on was of better taste than a fresh birthday cake that along with tastes better than the Eucharist's sweet-warm's icing. It wasn't long before they bumped into some turtle worms, half-fish maggots, and jackrabbit/ maggots, as if antagonism after antagonism during the grand cataclysm never would be a country that hadn't banned absinthe's. Watering of tastebuds, eats, with no feat of fertile incubation, but fitted as a road's non-concrete sewage drain, offered meals of fatal meats, in no need of thermal insulation, much different's canned-spray foamed-on polyurethane. In light of their dwindlin' shipwreck, an eyesight away there was a shack-jumbo-paddle-boat; in spite of their disgustment in heck, allied by one trait, teamed-up, they had approached, and afloat. There was Wood Duck Gal, Man, Girl & Boy; there was Woodchuck Gal, Man, Girl, and Boy. There was Wood Duck Woodchuck Man, there was Wood Duck Woodchuck Gal. One pet was a wood-duck-bodied pet wood duck woodchuck, one pet was a woodchuck-bodied wood duck woodchuck. They used to pay huge dues, stoopedly, to the bat frosted sasquatches, as unbalanced slash much maddened units in unison. Not making a stink alike besties getting to, bounded by chain links, on a deal they inked of binds, tempting plenty to down, inclined, day-drinks. Man, they in pride, had zero damn queue-phobics, and taken line-castings more than nootropics. As they tailed real far away, braced, the ligergiraffe, was pulled through the liquid, death-gripped with his limb; at straightway the aqua trailway's reliers were fab, fumbled to each ill-willed Blendedganism. There, there; there's where there were breeders, peep-pedes, half-sir flatworms, drastic earthworm dragons, maggot dragons, batbull vampwolves, the minion batrats, and the ghastly equippedly-sworded half-millipede bullock dragon. The scene beat a zoo much in hard-penned girth, not stuffed animals by hunting prey but no, zoo-food served, in-dang-house in the darkened lake's outskirts; the being, a two-hundred-yard stretchworth on, much-planted, all sides of the lake, was home to numerous clay mounds in the hardened-clay outers. Like a big dodge, by weighing bull, benched, the hiders sure had a wise critique, some hide-shack eased the dream team, sidelining toxins, its inners soothed them 'n' posed a hailed severage; while hangin' on by a single clench, the ligergiraffe played hide 'n' seek, sometimes lacking the freaking bright flight-response is similar to beggin' for a brain hemorrhage. The wood duck woodchuck clan's trusty threshold really crossed them as brawn, not a tid-dang-bit like pussies, their healths without veggies beat gunk, not with, un-burned, a vegan sandwich; the wood duck woodchuck clan, undetectably keen, dropped them off knowin' they in time would reach the exit-out ending the aquatic, subterranean passage. Hoo-ha, honored, did ban ruts, the hooked-up foot of the band upheld, but it had barred having to bolt down, to Swanocerosman what the wood duck wood chuck themed-clan was then's what it's that R & B's to Motown. The bear bull werewolf's lair lied where there was a bedward ingrown temperate zone, not a soul there knew near was light-type yellow, explosive, cold, brimstone. Entitled in-miles, lakeside, they stride, tread on, then cautiously yet not exhaustedly spot a log dang viny-topped, ivy-topped, cabin and bridge. Bein' within structured wood when vacant, yes so like (as), empty scholastic auditoriums; feeded (if misunderstood get a hint), scents more like bad threats reached of than whiffed bomb-emporiums. Liberative in inwards of minutes, the striped urged giraffe-part-marked ligergiraffe plus slashed, unlatched; freeing the clawed groundhog-hawk, sphinx lynx, and the dandy ligergiraffe's loved half-of that's the smilin'-big, turned-glad, free lionessgergiraffe. Yo, there was some metal-cage-roofed cellar that of which seats inwards, the hardened slash clay-based floor; soared, the lunge, 'twas vengeful, 'n' it made phew-yellers act ductiley, differently started than placed-claymores. The thick-haired bear bull werewolf busted through the door on his lair's end of the cabin's wooden, not glazed-wicker, transittin' bridge; when prior Swanocerosman and Goosepotomuswoman heard the crossway caught weight as if what the realm-meister for a fact did put in's not a river pass' brick bridge. The second the ligergiraffe heard the noise he dodged all not of the house due to being such a freaking keen sensor of okayed vantages, it was then he knew his every loved one getting out of this one would be difficult unlike somebody makin' in-place, needy fellers some homemade sandwiches. All of the momentum coming Swanocerosman and Goosepotamuswoman's way was enough to send them all through the opposite wall from which it came from, of the softened log cabin; Swanocerosman countered the bear bull werewolf by spinning him around by the shoulders right after he quickly-enough, managed to fling Goosepotamuswoman away from the collision like doing so was safe as not-so-costless dog-zappin'. Swanocerosman then used all his summoned strength to project it upwards towards a non-feeble rock-mock-icicle; before and after its very much chicken-hearted plus pigeon-hearted collapse, it dealt with sharpness more than one lapsed time like a chomped on, green, dope, non-hot, sliced pickle. The bear bull werewolf laid dead on a re-cently red, much-spiky miniature rock-mock-iceberg, some story; like his log two-door's deceased as a mall's food-court's feast's meats, what doesn't in the hands of a till-the-end-of-time-beaten brother lie's purgatory. Not beat like a victorious plus boxed boxer, jolly's what they were made because of their not so inglorious plump onslaughter. The burnt x-eds, bled out, not quite like by-months troubled madams; creatures bent, let out, not bye-byes, final muscle spasms. With breath too, yes, all teetered and rowdy slash as linked was integrally-labeled, naval, panting, war-bourne, sunken admirals. When rock chest-rocked the bullwolf-werebear, forthcoming like the prefix which's circum; it meant to them all the world, that's how their last clash resulted, sinfully the bear bull werewolf badly broke both of his clavicles, then rock went not before being shorn from the spiky ceilin', in his sternum.

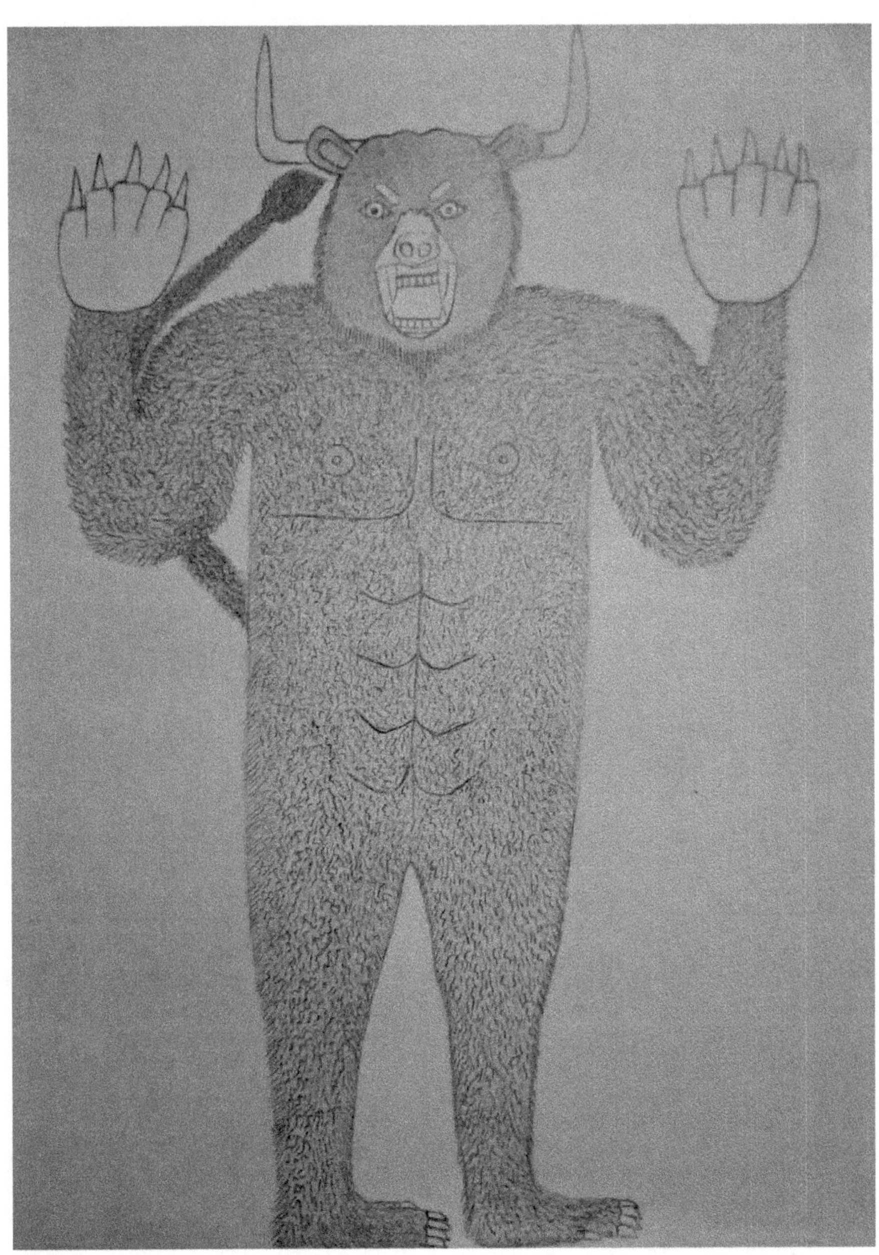

Bear Bull Werewolf

Jackrabbit Slash Maggot & Worm Turtle

The Equippedly-Sworded Half Millipede Bullock Dragon, Maggot Dragon, Peep-Pede, Half-Sir Flatworm, Drastic Earthworm Dragon, Batbull Vampwolf, & Batrat

Sphynx Lynx & Clawed Groundhog-Hawk

Lionessgergiraffe

Swanocerosman Versus Bear Bull Werewolf

# CHAPTER NINE:
# ANIMANVILLE

Once back at ground level, hunter and gatherer panther sirs guided them to where the lionessgergiraffe was a guardian angel, Swanocerosman's clan all recieved the Medal of Nestled Love, it was just unalike it'd be to include farting with facials. At least Swanocerosman's face hadn't had spit in it different from the tip of a real-recently used-up bugle; the hunter and gatherer panther sirs' authority back home since their last golden line of defense was rescued sure'd give the loved rescuers, each a key to their adorn city, and so it was a moment commemorated via their newspaper which went by the name of The Useful Newsful. The civilization's newcomers were given much: big ups, one mansion, and paninis, they received commendation from chipmonkish monks, plus policegeese. Swanocerosman and Goosepotamuswoman were brought to play card games with the members of the royal house, they loved when it was unfinished like some innin' void of outs. King Swan and Queen Swan, Prince & Princess Goose, The Gerbilly Earl and The Cow-Chick Countess, Duke Goose, The Elephant Femme Duchess, The Ferret Baron, The Parrotish Baroness, and The Leopard Jester were termed all oligarchs. In martini glasses their martini man fixed them hard cardamom vodka and citrus mint gin, in glass bowls they had all-natural slash chopped-up hibiscus licorice as well as cinnamon licorice. It was different from the wilderness as Queen Swan was pettin' the swangoose, & King Swan was pettin' the swangoose mongoose. Adept they played craps, slots, pai gow, mahjong, poker, Animanish roulette, blackjack, and also baccarat; to usuals dude what else must've been straight sad at all's when some guy's out-hotdogged, for sure gas-filled, hexed, misused, dead-ran-half-ass, auto had one flat. Swanocerosman and Goosepotamuswoman got a mighty hang of it where and when it counted like non-poopy newbies, it seemed like they couldn't do wrong different from bad kids whose actions made sure they each got ruby booties. The only played game they played that differed relative to how it so's on earth all across the whole balled world, was Animanish Roulette. The crew's rules were all losers were who were, had to take care of the winner's pet, splittin' the task-list, until a declared-in-full numerical amount of times elapses; it was that way since they dug funnies plus it took money and bein' Animanish to bet. Swanocerosman was in luck nonstop as much as it was difficult to give the stork-upine a backscratch, he couldn't stop talkin' about eats once he got back to his new abode to corkscrew, fry eggs and latch, onto his woohed counterpart romantically. He felt as if his crazy days had became a newfound sure-garbled antiquity. Someone restored peace for relevant, mid it, Blendedganisms, sized much alike some damn clap-backer, & the in-deep had grimaced; they fully cared warmly since bigger-ness wins interest like some liked-up "fact-pageant" news column. Mallard Man's been their semi-filthy city's pacifist, like what Batman is to Gotham. Toucan Newt Man treated the sweet city like a booze slash food stand. All night there were all types of cheers plus beers, blood orange mimosas, hard dark chocolate coquitos, and raw-mint mojitos; where what's been fridging's where the tied peep-like three really couldn't stop sweetly appreciating their new quarters' amenities. Also, the non-low-key, angst-less banquet's offers offered dandelion root spirytus, and agave sake as well as wasabi sake. Half the time murmuring, nobody was squarer, though, than a rhombus, and their lines were sterling; no, nothing was full way or half-way pompous. Non-stopped Huracans, tow-trucks, too Range Rovers 'n' such, ain't vocal (lingual) much as 'em; Swanoce-rosman's clan woke up to hangovers, it was a totally fun bo-nanza. Marked of gladness witnessed, straight different so's chemo, far from an incriminatin' imbroglio. It was pleasant to the senses (tailored-kosher) 'n' more personably than the

aurora borealis; like bein' in a bungalow the way they weren't
gettin' sun-soaked, with some splendid ruly census, they were
motor-skill posers, involving as we suppose, opposing laby-
rinths.

Chipmonkish Monks, Lynx Peep, Panther Slash Sir, Mole Man, Grass-hopper Man, & Ant Man

Mallard Man

The Policegeese

Prince Goose & Princess Goose

King Swan & Queen Swan

The Royals

## EPILOGUE: UM, HUH?

Herein hearty heroism darn near potioned a hero in addition
to his heroine.  Getting out of the mayhem and into where
they'd be less concerned about defense mechanisms headin'
in-full through a brainstem, was the reason bein' eased differently from caught cons; meant served-up's stellar nectar, one
sweetened perfectly, no long johns. Basin' real natively like a
suburb's name's treatment, they're with needs, famously, like
a color gradient.

www.ingramcontent.com/pod-product-compliance
Lightning Source LLC
Chambersburg PA
CBHW052101150726
48002CB00002B/976